Elk and Wolf

Elk and Wolf

By DC Fidler and Travis Teffner

DCFidler Publishing
<2017>

Published by DCFidler Publishing
1117 University Avenue, #505
Morgantown, WV 26505
DCFidlerpublishing@gmail.com

Printed in the United States of America
by Lulu Press, Inc.

This play is entirely a work of fiction.
Any resemblance to actual persons, living or dead,
is entirely coincidental.

ISBN: 978-0-9989729-2-3
Library of Congress Control Number: 2017911794

Acknowledgments

DC Fidler

A heartfelt thank you to the following friends, colleagues, and mentors:

- Travis Teffner for sharing the emotional roller-coaster journey with me as we explored strong characters in extraordinary circumstances. What a pleasure to create with you my friend.
- My amazing writing professors at the University of North Carolina at Chapel Hill: Doris Betts, Max Steele, Wallace Kaufman, John Parker, and writers-in-residence professors, James Dickey and Robert Anderson. All I have to do is stroll through the Carolina campus, and your warming and challenging presences stir my soul.

Travis Adam Teffner

- DC Fidler, thank you for your endless support and sharing your time, tremendous heart, and talent with me.
- RJ Casey, thank you for your consultations not only on this play, but life.

Elk and Wolf premiered on February 1, 2013 at M. T. Pockets Theatre, Morgantown, West Virginia.

Cast

AGENT TREVOR WOLF	*Travis Teffner*
BAILEY CAULFIELD ROSS	*Sean Marko*
AGENT MARGARET FINCH	*Mya Brown*
TEANNA WOLF	*Shannon Uphold*
SERGEANT MARLOW	*Issac Synder*
NEWSCASTER AUDIO	*Ben Adducchio*

Producers	*Toni Morris*
	Vicki Trickett
Director	*Donald Fidler*
Assistant Director	*Jonathan Lazzell*
Light-Sound Design	*Jonathan Lazzell*
Military Consultants	*Major RJ Casey*
Scene and Prop Crew	*Jonathan Lazzell*
	Eduardo Cole
	Colin Crawford
	Tawyna Drake
	Romero Cottingham

Characters

AGENT TREVOR WOLF
BAILEY CAULFIELD ROSS
AGENT MARGARET FINCH
TEANNA WOLF
SERGEANT MARLOW
NEWSCASTER AUDIO

Note

In contrast to formal scripts for use in rehearsals, this is a
book of the script, containing more stage directions to aid
readers to envision what can be happening upon the stage.
Most actors prefer few or no directions, allowing them to
discover and create the lives of their characters.

Settings

Both sets are in the Washington DC area in July of present year.

1. A Homeland Security (Federal) Interrogation Room with a smaller Observation Room that has a one-way mirror/window for observations of interrogations. One door connects the two rooms via a small anteroom. The Observation Room also has a door to the outside. The Interrogation room has a jail door that goes to the cells and buzzes each time before it is opens and each time after it closes. A digital clock sits high in the wall of the Interrogation Room. The Interrogation Room has one interrogation type lamp hanging from the ceiling and a microphone hanging from the ceiling. Sign on wall of Interrogation Room states, "No electronics, No food, No ID badges, No weapons or sharp objects."
2. The living room of Agent Trevor Wolf which has a couch, chairs, coat rack, and a television along with other optional furniture. There is a coat closet, a door to the outside, and a staircase to an upper floor.

Note: Names of the Secretary of Homeland Security and the Secretary of Health and Human Services may be updated when appropriate.

Elk and Wolf
Act One · Scene One

Lights rise from black to having only the overhead interrogation lamp lighting the Interrogation Room and full lighting in the Observation Room. "15:20" displays on the large digital wall clock. The rooms are empty of people.

TREVOR enters the Observation Room, unpacks, places his face against the one-way mirror/window to look into the Interrogation Room, but it is too dark to see. He makes certain no one can see him and then walks into Interrogation Room. He turns on the light switch and full lighting lights the Interrogation Room. He places his face against the mirror/window and realizes he cannot see into the Observation Room. He looks around with a child-like curiosity, touching the furniture and then he sits at the table. When he hears the jail-style door buzz, he abruptly stands and returns to the Observation Room.

MARLOW and BAILEY enter the Interrogation Room. MARLOW wears an Army combat uniform with a military police tag. BAILEY is in an orange jump suit with handcuffs and foot cuffs. He stands by chair at table, stretching as MARLOW stands guard at parade rest in his usual spot.

FINCH enters the Observation Room, nods to greet TREVOR, then pulls off her identification badge, FBI badge, and wedding ring, placing her ID on a rack and her badge and ring in a box. She glances at a report and walks into the Interrogation Room. She paces as she reads.

BAILEY continues stretching by the table.

FINCH: *(Firmly.)* Sit!

(BAILEY frowns and sits.)

FINCH: *(Paces as thumbs through report.)* You were taking photographs from the top of the hill.

BAILEY: Video.

FINCH: Video from the top of the hill. A Shell station.

BAILEY: The explosion.

FINCH: The Sugar Grove Shell Station. One car blew up, causing one gas pump to explode. No injuries.

BAILEY: No injuries.

FINCH: You videoed the police cars, ambulances, and TV crew examining the site.

BAILEY: Yes ma'am.

FINCH: Then the local police spotted you and walked up the hill to talk with you.

BAILEY: I had to wave my hands before they spotted me. Two local deputies. One made it to the top of the hill. The other officer was . . . weight-challenged.

FINCH: Did they ask why you made a video?

BAILEY: The smaller officer did.

FINCH: Have a seat Sergeant.
(Mumbles.)
We may be here a while.

(MARLOW sits.)

FINCH: What did the officers do next?

BAILEY: The officer radioed other officers from the explosion site. They hiked up, handcuffed me, and transported me to the Watauga County Sheriff's Office.

FINCH: Boone. North Carolina mountains. Beautiful place.

BAILEY: Mountains, lakes, sure. If you're into that kind of thing.

FINCH: The reason you gave for blowing up the gas pump . . .
(Reads from report.)
"The Sugar Grove Shell Station attendant gave me a disgruntled look when I informed her that the men's toilet was dirty."

BAILEY: Disgustingly. "Disgustingly dirty."

FINCH: Pardon me, yes. "Disgustingly dirty."
(Reads to herself, then speaks.)
C4 plastic explosive.

BAILEY: Accurate. Black market.

FINCH: I see that. "I bought C4 on the black market. Expensive but I am wealthy."

BAILEY: That makes me sound like a snob. I only meant that I am capable.

FINCH: Capable.

BAILEY: Not a snob, but that I have an easy means.

FINCH: And the reason they transferred you to Homeland Security?

BAILEY: Extraordinary rendition, took me across jurisdictions.

FINCH: Extraordinary? Uh-huh.

BAILEY: I warned them: there will be additional sites. Your report appears accurate.

FINCH: Accurate is good. Your name is accurate, age is accurate. No fingerprints on file. The car you blew up was registered to you. First car you owned. Only two months. "Bailey Caulfield Ross. Tuxedo, New York." Tuxedo? Like the uh . . .

BAILEY: Like the suits. The suits were named after the town. Tuxedo was first a Native-American name for the lake that's there. Then the town took that name.

FINCH: Did not know that. "First-year law student at Duke University."

BAILEY: I dropped out two months ago.

FINCH: Dropped out?

BAILEY: I learned enough.

FINCH: Enough?

BAILEY: Enough to prepare me.

FINCH: "Enough," "Capable" . . . For doing what?

BAILEY: Whatever arises.

FINCH: Uh huh.
(Closes report.)
Tell you what. I have a forensics intern working, studying with me. I want you to talk with my intern.

BAILEY: I don't want to talk with your intern. This is serious.

FINCH: Very serious.

BAILEY: I won't waste my time with an intern.

FINCH: Help me out. I have to grade this young man.

BAILEY: No. I want to confer with . . . with . . .

FINCH: With a lawyer?

BAILEY: I tried calling my lawyer. He was neither in his office, at home, nor on his mobile.

FINCH: Mobile?

BAILEY: Cell phone. I want to talk with someone else.

FINCH: Who? My boss?

BAILEY: Absolutely. I want to talk with him.

FINCH: *She* doesn't want to talk with you. *She* thinks they should have kept you at the Watauga County Sheriff's Office.

BAILEY: That's bullshit.

FINCH: You'd be amazed how much C4 is floating around out there. We had a farmer blow off his hand exploding a beaver dam. One month before you blew up a gas pump.

BAILEY: This is more than a beaver's dam. I had an ingenious detonator.

FINCH: Help'em out a little. Between you and me? He's not that good.

BAILEY: No.

FINCH: Tell'im what you told me. Make up something. See if he can ascertain that you're lying.
(Gathers papers and exits.)

BAILEY: *(Yells after Finch.)* I won't speak with your intern!

(MARLOW stands.)

FINCH: *(Once inside Anteroom, yells.)* What a waste of resources! *(Enters Observation Room.)* Trevor? Anything yet on this "capable" guy's parents?

TREVOR: *(Looking at computer.)* Fulmer just updated Mr. Ross' file. His parents are in Borneo, SCUBA diving and sailing. Flying home tomorrow in their private jet.

FINCH: They should finish their holiday, let their "capable" law-student son sit and pout that we don't take him seriously.

TREVOR: His father is CEO of a military contract company. Worth hundreds of millions. His mother has a law degree but never practiced. She came from three generations of New York City Construction tycoons. Worth more than her husband . . . and Mr. Ross is adopted and he . . .

FINCH: A clean-cut, millionaire's *adopted* kid blew up a little gas pump. Sleep deprivation, white noise, a hood, isolation, sodium amytal . . . nothing . . . Okay, you watched me interview a real terrorist last week. Show me what you learned.

TREVOR: With this guy?

FINCH: Rapport building skills.

TREVOR: And you'll grade me, based on *this* guy?

FINCH: Dumb it down a bit. He's not too bright.

TREVOR: He was tops in his law school class.

FINCH: Emotionally he's a two-year old.

TREVOR: *(Mumbles.)* "Dumb it down."
(Walks toward Interrogation Room.)

FINCH: Wait!
(Snaps fingers.)
Take off that ID and badge. And that wedding ring. No pens or sharp pencils either.
(She takes TREVOR'S pens, ID, badge, and ring, hanging ID on rack and placing rings and badge in box.)

TREVOR: What do I write with?

(FINCH hands TREVOR a box of Crayola Crayons.)

TREVOR: Crayolas? Is this protocol?

FINCH: My protocol. Ever since I got this scar on my cheek.

TREVOR: Oh God. A detainee stabbed you?

FINCH: My sister's daughter. I was babysitting. Amelia's meaner than any detainee.

TREVOR: *(Takes handful of crayons and puts them in his jacket pocket. Speaks as exits.)* Babysitting. That's what I'm ordered to do. Babysit.
(Pauses at door to compose, then enters Interrogation Room. Spills a couple of crayons on floor and stoops and picks them up.)

(BAILEY breathes slowly and loudly like a fire dragon while staring intensely at TREVOR.)

(TREVOR pauses as he is afraid to approach, but cautiously approaches a couple of steps.)

(BAILEY breaths like a dragon again.)

(TREVOR backs up and pauses again.)

BAILEY: *(Suddenly forms both hands into a pistol pointed at TREVOR and yells.)* Pow!!!

(TREVOR jumps.)

BAILEY: *(Mumbles.)* Jesus.
(Sneers, looks at MARLOW and shakes head as if saying, "What an idiot.")

TREVOR: Hi. I'm Tracker.

BAILEY: Tracker? Tracker? What kind of name is—

TREVOR: Nickname. We aren't allowed to use given names.

BAILEY: I told your teacher, supervisor, whoever, I'm not speaking with you. Nothing personal.

TREVOR: Oh. I thought she said you agreed.

BAILEY: You're shitting me. No! . . . Sorry. That sounded mean. I want you to get your good grade. But use someone else as your test subject.

TREVOR: Who?

BAILEY: There are other people you can interview?

TREVOR: Not really. Business is slow.

BAILEY: "Business is slow." I'm the only person in Homeland Security you can interview?

TREVOR: That's what she said.

BAILEY: Shit . . . Fine. Five minutes.

TREVOR: I'm supposed to interview ten.

BAILEY: Shit. Eight minutes.

TREVOR: *(Hesitates, then sits.)* Okay.
(Arranges notebooks and crayons overly neatly on desk.)

BAILEY: *(Stares at Trevor's arranging and shakes head before speaking.)* Do I have to stay in these handcuffs?

TREVOR: I don't know.

BAILEY: You don't know?

TREVOR: Should I go ask?

BAILEY: What do you know?

TREVOR: You blew up something.

BAILEY: Something?

TREVOR: My supervisor told me, but I can't understand her when she mumbles.

BAILEY: A service station.

TREVOR: Didn't sound like she mumbled, "service station."

BAILEY: Filling station?

TREVOR: Uh . . . Maybe "filling." Or "fillin'."
(Snaps fingers.)
No. "Gas pump." She said. "He blew up a little gas pump."

BAILEY: Jesus. You already used up one minute.

TREVOR: *(Writes in notebook.)* "Filling station."

BAILEY: Two minutes.

TREVOR: Two?

BAILEY: Counting the time you took to organize your book and coloring crayons.

TREVOR: I didn't know you started timing . . . Why a "filling station?"

BAILEY: Good second question. To get attention, "Tracker".

TREVOR: *(Writes in notebook.)* "To get attention."

BAILEY: Jesus. Look buddy—

TREVOR: Tracker.

BAILEY: Tracker.

TREVOR: What my grandfather called me.

BAILEY: Okay, Tracker. I'll help you. Don't write down my answers. Remember what I say and write that down later. You'll learn more. Trust me on this. I'm a law student.

TREVOR: *(Writes.)* "A law student."

BAILEY: No. Stop writing. Ask, listen, and remember. Jesus. Three minutes and I know more about you than you know about me.

TREVOR: You know about me?

(*BAILEY nods to MARLOW for permission to get cup of water. MARLOW reluctantly nods.*)

BAILEY: (*Stands and walks to bench and pours himself a cup of water as he talks.*) You're a forensic graduate intern. You were close to your grandfather, who nicknamed you with what sounds like a Native American type name, or a deep-South-hunting type name. I'll go with the former. So, you probably have weaponry skills. You obsessively, compulsively line up your crayons and notebook, probably everything in your closet and drawers. Am I right?

TREVOR: I don't like messy.

BAILEY: You don't like "messy." You probably hunt, right? Wrong? Name like Tracker?

TREVOR: Since I was little.

BAILEY: See how much I know. You don't see me writing. (*Sits.*)

TREVOR: You're in handcuffs.

BAILEY: Even out of handcuffs I would not be writing.

TREVOR: But you could.

BAILEY: Trust me on this, Tracker. I'm a law student.

TREVOR: In handcuffs.

BAILEY: Do handcuffs make you better than I?

TREVOR: Makes you less comfortable than me.

BAILEY: I . . .
(Laughs.)
Yes. Yes it does. Makes me "less comfortable." No more writing? Deal?

TREVOR: While you were lecturing me, you used up some of my minutes.

BAILEY: I did. I did. I apologize. I'll add on . . . one minute.

TREVOR: Two?

BAILEY: Okay, sure. Two.

TREVOR: I forgot your answer.

BAILEY: See? And you wrote down my last answer.

(TREVOR looks at notebook.)

BAILEY: No, no, you can do this. What was your question?

TREVOR: Uh . . . "Why a filling station?"

BAILEY: And I answered?

TREVOR: "To get attention."

BAILEY: Good job. See? Now close your notebook. Lay down your coloring crayon.

TREVOR: *(Closes notebook and places crayon on desk.)* What kind of attention?

BAILEY: The kind of attention people most crave.

TREVOR: Love?

BAILEY: No, well, that's important too, yes. But I was thinking: people taking one seriously. Believing one's ideas.

TREVOR: Who?

BAILEY: Another good question, Tracker. People who have the power, the capability to take action upon one's ideas.

TREVOR: Your parents?

BAILEY: Uh, when we were younger, yes. Accurate. But now that we're older? People who direct, who lead.

TREVOR: Filling station managers?

BAILEY: Tracker, Tracker, if you want a good grade? And I'm sure you do, buddy. Step back. Look at the big picture.

TREVOR: Shell Oil?

BAILEY: How do you know it was a Shell station?

TREVOR: Ms. . . . I mean, my supervisor said, "Shell," then I must not have understood "fillin'" or maybe she said, "little *Shell* gas pump."

BAILEY: Okay, okay. Tracker? Do you believe if one steals a tube of Colgate whitening toothpaste from a Walmart, that person has something against Colgate? Or against Walmart? Or that—

TREVOR: Maybe that person needs to brush his teeth.

BAILEY: Okay Tracker. Or? Attention from?

TREVOR: Big picture?

BAILEY: Bigger.

(TREVOR nods.)

BAILEY: Okay. Got it? Hold onto that thought.

(TREVOR nods.)

BAILEY: Good. Now take that specific thought, and think even bigger.

TREVOR: Okay.

BAILEY: Got it?

(TREVOR nods.)

BAILEY: What do you have?

TREVOR: The President of the United States.

BAILEY: Kind of a big leap on that last one, don't you think, buddy?

TREVOR: You said, "Bigger than big."

BAILEY: I did, yes, I did . . . but, let's go for something uh . . . something more abstract.

TREVOR: Abstract?
(Looks up at microphone and whispers so FINCH cannot hear.)
Uh . . . What's more abstract?

BAILEY: Probably no *one* correct answer, but I was thinking something like, civilizations. People collectively who don't take seriously that less fortunate people do without. Not Jean Val Jean in *Les Miserable*, stealing a loaf of bread because he was hungry, but existing more at a mythological level. Let's say . . . Robin Hood.

TREVOR: Stealing from the rich to give to the poor?

BAILEY: People knew Robin Hood was serious about social discrepancies.

TREVOR: But you don't steal. You blow stuff up.

BAILEY: Hold on Tracker, hold on buddy. We're getting there.

TREVOR: You're going to steal from the rich? Give to the—

BAILEY: Level the field a bit.

TREVOR: Holy shit.
(Walks to MARLOW and without letting BAILEY see, motions for MARLOW to leave. MARLOW reluctantly exits.)

BAILEY: Impressive, huh? Now. When you leave me, write that up. Give that to your supervisor, Ms. Mrs. . . .

TREVOR: I 'm not allowed to say her name.

BAILEY: I guarantee you a good grade.

TREVOR: I need a good grade.

BAILEY: Where are you from?

TREVOR: Wyoming.

BAILEY: Wyoming? I ski the Grand Tetons. Holy shit majestic. My dad hunted there but he parked me in the lodge with our au pair. Same with little outposts all over Vermont.
(Mumbles with disgust.)
Little unimpressive municipal airports.

TREVOR: I miss Wyoming.

BAILEY: You said you hunted?

TREVOR: With my grandpa.

BAILEY: Buffalo?

TREVOR: *What?*

BAILEY: Sorry. Guess I read too many—

TREVOR: Elk, moose, deer.

BAILEY: Wolfs?

TREVOR: Wolves.

BAILEY: Wolves.

TREVOR: No, wolf is my . . . I like wolves.

BAILEY: Part Native American. I was on target.

TREVOR: How did you deduce that?

BAILEY: Nickname "Tracker?" A hunch. I mean, I could be right; I could be wrong. One takes chances like that as a lawyer. Same in forensics? Hunches? . . . Sorry I was rude, pushy about your notebook and crayons.

TREVOR: I'm doing better without them.

BAILEY: *(Looks up at ceiling mic and then whispers.)* I didn't like your supervisor. So many people who don't get it.

TREVOR: *(Whispers.)* Get what?

BAILEY: Get people. Did your grandfather get people, understand people?

TREVOR: *(Long pause.)* He was quiet . . . watched, listened.

BAILEY: My parents talk all the time. Don't see, don't hear. I strive to not be like them. Too often I am.

TREVOR: It's all right.

BAILEY: No. No it's not all right. You gave me your insightful answer and I did not take you seriously. I did in my head, but I did not show you that courtesy, respect.
(Extends hand to shake hands.)
I apologize.

TREVOR: *(Does not shake hands.)* Apology accepted.

BAILEY: Huh.
(Pauses to think.)

TREVOR: What?

BAILEY: Just wondering what that would feel like if my parents apologized for doing to me what I did to you. Then I could say, "Apology accepted."

TREVOR: Won't happen?

BAILEY: Not even on our deathbeds.

TREVOR: Whoa.
(Pauses.)
You still want them to take you seriously?

BAILEY: I moved on. Far on. I want . . .
(Yells to ceiling mic.)
seriousness from others!

TREVOR: Bigger than big . . . Is it okay . . . okay for me to ask
. . .

BAILEY: From whom?

(TREVOR nods.)

BAILEY: *(Whispers.)* Off the record? Not for your "school report?" Just between you and me?

FINCH: *(Turns up speaker volume control on wall.)*

(TREVOR nods.)

BAILEY: Crazy as this is going to sound? You were dead on target and I did not acknowledge it . . . The President of the United States.

TREVOR: Holy shit.

BAILEY: And Congress.

TREVOR: Congress?

(FINCH looks at her beeper and then makes phone call.)

BAILEY: You must think I'm grandiose, narcissistic, delusional, psychotic? No. Years and years of thinking this through . . . You don't believe me.

TREVOR: My eyes are open. My ears are open.

BAILEY: Like your grandfather.
(Pauses, then looks at clock on wall.)

TREVOR: Is my time up?

BAILEY: Seven minutes ago.
(*Should base number of minutes on real time on clock.)

TREVOR: You went overtime with me.

BAILEY: Something feels familiar.

TREVOR: It does.

BAILEY: Feelings have a way of knowing beyond what we know.

TREVOR: Hm.

BAILEY: *(Closes eyes as if staring up at sun.)* If I close my eyes, I almost picture our being friends, kid friends, riding up that ride at Disneyland with fake snow on top.

TREVOR: The Matterhorn.

BAILEY: "The Matterhorn." High up. Looking over the park. Sharing, not knowing what lies ahead of us.

(TREVOR closes eyes and imagines ride.)

(FINCH hangs up phone and taps on mirror/window.)

TREVOR: My supervisor.

BAILEY: Guess I granted you more time than your own supervisor. Good luck with that grade, Tracker.

(TREVOR packs up notebooks and crayons calmly, and summons MARLOW to room. MARLOW enters Interrogation Room.)

TREVOR: *(Extends hand to BAILEY.)* Thank you for helping me.

(BAILEY smiles and then shakes hands.)

TREVOR: *(Enters Observation Room.)* What's up?

FINCH: Three more Shell stations blew. Ninety minutes ago. Tampa, Florida. Outside Rock Hill, South Carolina, and Cheyenne, Wyoming.

TREVOR: Cheyenne? All of them were ninety minutes ago?

FINCH: Two, three minutes apart. This time, a grandmother and her seven-year-old grandson were trapped in one of the cars. Burned.
(Hands folder to Trevor.)
Here are the faxed photos.

(TREVOR looks at photos and reacts. TREVOR and FINCH walk to mirror/window and stare at BAILEY as they talk.)

FINCH: He said there would be other sites.

TREVOR: Car bombs?

FINCH: No car at the pumps in Tampa.

TREVOR: Cell-phone-trigger detonators.

FINCH: Crossed state lines. Federal case. Transportation of explosives.

TREVOR: Weapons of mass destruction.

FINCH: Domestic terrorism . . . murder. Possibly the death penalty.

TREVOR: All Shell stations?

FINCH: All Shell.

TREVOR: C4 explosives?

FINCH: TEDAC is confirming. I think we can bet on C4.

TREVOR: Did he use a cell-phone-trigger detonator in the first car bomb in North Carolina?

FINCH: That is confirmed.

TREVOR: Where was our Mr. Bailey Ross ninety minutes ago?

FINCH: Calling his lawyer.

TREVOR: You're shitting me.

FINCH: *(Disbelieving.)* You don't think . . . Damn!
(Picks up phone.)
Rinehart? Do you have the number Mr. Ross called when he called his lawyer?
(Pause.)
Uh huh.
(Places hand over phone receiver to talk to Trevor.)
Rinehart dialed for him, three numbers. His lawyer never answered at any of the three numbers.
(Into the phone.)
Give me those numbers . . . uh, wait, slow down.

(TREVOR pulls out his mobile phone, and looking over FINCH'S shoulder, dials a number she wrote. FINCH pauses to frown at TREVOR for breaking protocol by using his mobile phone.)

FINCH: Okay. Exactly what was the time on each? . . . I see.
(Ends call.)

TREVOR: *(Waits for answer.)* Straight to voice mail. No recorded voice.

FINCH: *(Stares at BAILEY, pauses.)* All on my watch.

(TREVOR joins FINCH to observe BAILEY.)

FINCH: You skipping the barbeque Saturday?

TREVOR: And miss your Cuban cheese-coated corn on the cob? Please.

FINCH: Are you counting on Teanna and the rest of us women to do all the cooking?

TREVOR: I cook . . . can I be Bailey's case agent?

FINCH: This guy's case agent? . . . If I closely supervise you? A possibility.

(TREVOR hurries toward Interrogation Room.)

FINCH: Wait! . . . This guy connects with you, but get smarter with him. You know that ground-rules speech I give? Take charge. Lay that on him.

TREVOR: *(Nods, enters Interrogation Room, stands.)* Cellphone-trigger detonators?

BAILEY: You're quick for an intern, Tracker.

TREVOR: A grandmother and her seven—

(FINCH pounds loudly on mirror/window.)

TREVOR: *(Holds hand toward the mirror/window, gesturing, "Stop.")* A grandmother and her seven-year-old grandson burned to death.
(Shows photos to BAILEY.)

BAILEY: *(Sickened by photos.)* I feared more deaths than two. No deaths would be better.

TREVOR: Know this Bailey Caulfield Ross. I am with the FBI and I will be your case agent.

BAILEY: My CA? Quite a promotion, Tracker.

TREVOR: Listen! I will be your only friend, your only connection to the world.
(Talks to ceiling mic.)
May we please have that clock off?

(FINCH frowns and shakes head. Turns power off to the digital clock.)

TREVOR: Thank you.
(To Bailey.)
You will talk with me and only me. Not even with that guard. The FBI identified you as murdering US Citizens with terrorist weapons of mass destruction. There are others who work here who are not as patient as I, who right or wrong will do what they want with you. Do not waste my time. Do not insult my superiors. You *will* tell me what I want to know. Guard? You can leave us.

MARLOW: Uh . . . I let protocol slip the first time. I need clearance.

TREVOR: I'm his case agent now.

MARLOW: Uh . . . Okay. Yes sir.
(Exits.)

BAILEY: I do not even get to know the time. Shit, Tracker. Not for a grade anymore, huh? Guess now I'm an HVT.

TREVOR: High value target? Was that your goal?

BAILEY: Your superiors should take me seriously.

TREVOR: My reports go high. Do we have an understanding?

BAILEY: I have a dream.

TREVOR: Do we have an understanding?

BAILEY: Yes! We have an understanding. Now as I was saying, I have a dream.

TREVOR: A dream. Martin Luther King was shot for having a dream.

BAILEY: But now, we have a Martin Luther King Day, a Martin Luther King Memorial, had a black President.

TREVOR: Your dream?

BAILEY: Health care.

TREVOR: Health care?

BAILEY: Chances at life.

TREVOR: We have Presidents and Congress who pass bills for that sort of thing.

BAILEY: Incoherent and insufficient.

TREVOR: Dr. King protested in a civil manner. You blew up four service stations, killing a grandmother and her seven-year-old grandson. What am I missing?

BAILEY: Oh, Tracker, you are an optimist. What? "Change we can believe in?" Add a pinch of pepper to a large pot of boiling water and declare, "Wow! What good soup!"

(FINCH knocks on mirror/window, but TREVOR holds up hand, "not yet.")

BAILEY: Let me ask you something.

TREVOR: Ask.

BAILEY: Could you sleep in the jungle without soap for days on end?

TREVOR: Soap?

BAILEY: Yes or no?

TREVOR: Depends on many factors such as—

BAILEY: Okay then, let's say you had no soap and were in the jungle where it was the rainy season so it rained for weeks on end and you had no sleep for days and your partners and you had no soap and there were lots of bugs. Would you mind having no soap?

TREVOR: Again, it would depend on many factors but—

BAILEY: Let's say you were alone in the rain forest and it was raining and you had an open-ended assignment and you had no shelter or if you weren't alone you didn't like the other people and you had no soap—"

(FINCH knocks on mirror/window much louder.)

TREVOR: Excuse me.
(Summons MARLOW, who enters Interrogation Room and stands guard. TREVOR exits to ante-room of Observation Room and screams.)
I hate those fuckin' soap questions!
(Calms self before entering Observation Room.)
Now what? Bailey has access to the questions on our psych evals?

FINCH: Need a donut?

TREVOR: You called me back here for a donut?

FINCH: Chocolate covered, raspberry, chocolate cream with or without sprinkles.

TREVOR: What are you eating?

FINCH: Maple frosted.

TREVOR: Give me a pinch of your donut.

(FINCH gives TREVOR a pinch of donut. He eats, takes a deep breath, and re-enters Interrogation Room. Pours self a cup of water.)

BAILEY: More updates?

TREVOR: Donuts. Some have sprinkles. Want me to get you one?
(Motions for MARLOW to leave and MARLOW exits.)

BAILEY: *(Makes disgusted face.)* How about loosening my cuffs?

TREVOR: No chance.

BAILEY: I guess that also means no more phone calls. And no soap.

TREVOR: You were in a top law school, the top of your class. Promise for every opportunity to change our world. Today with three phone calls you killed two people. Even got someone else to dial, do your dirty work.

BAILEY: Casualties.

TREVOR: Casualties? This is war?

BAILEY: Eight years ago, I declared war.

TREVOR: At fourteen? Who did you declare war on?

BAILEY: Whom? A society that allows children, old people, crippled people to die even though that society has more than ample means.

TREVOR: You kill children and old people. You're a fucking terrorist, Bailey. Left wing. Right wing. Idealist. Doesn't matter. A terrorist.

BAILEY: I liked you better when you needed a good grade.

TREVOR: More Shell stations? So, people will say, "Avoid Shell stations, avoid the pattern," and then *wham*! You break that pattern.

BAILEY: I imagine people from all levels of government are planning how to search every Shell station. How much time will that take? Who will manage long lines of traffic waiting for the "safe, already-cleaned" Shell stations?

TREVOR: Chaos.

BAILEY: Stock markets will take a hit. Sports events, vacations, concerts will be cancelled.

TREVOR: You sound disinterested in chaos.

BAILEY: One man shooting his gun on a Virginia Interstate outside of DC disrupted "business as usual."

TREVOR: Being isolated in here, you will not read about, nor hear about what happens.

BAILEY: Solitary confinement?
(Quiet chuckle.)
Age fourteen to eighteen, Tracker. You know how I spent my summer vacations? Every summer my parents sent me to a wilderness camp in Wisconsin. I persuaded them to let me ride there with "friends." Not dote over me. Let me go it alone like the big boy I was. And you know what,

Tracker? I never went to those camps. While my parents globetrotted with their like-minded friends, I rented myself a little cabin and placed myself into solitary confinement. One month, every summer, four years.

TREVOR: Your parents never checked on you?

BAILEY: I wasn't the warm-cuddly-type son.
(Imitates parents.)
"Bailey? You look relaxed, confident. Wilderness camp is a completing choice for you."

TREVOR: Your parents were not the warm-cuddly-type parents.

BAILEY: What limitations did your family have?

TREVOR: Not limitations that led me at age fourteen to plan Jihad.

BAILEY: I devised how to water board myself.

TREVOR: *(Laughs.)* How does "*one*" water board "*one's*" self, Bailey?

BAILEY: I almost drowned. If one relaxes, dampens, so-to-speak, the impulse to panic, one does not fear dying. In fifth grade, I did drown once. One of the ponds on our estate. My cousin revived me. I never told anyone that I elected to quit swimming. Wondered what inhaling my next breath under water would be like . . . Fantastically calming.

(TREVOR stares in silence.)

BAILEY: I was a weird child, the cute kid dressed up like a doll.

TREVOR: Living in a vacuum.

BAILEY: Wrong, Tracker. Way too many hugs, an abundance of gifts, standardized praise.

TREVOR: Who chooses self-imposed isolation?

BAILEY: Freaks?

TREVOR: Are you a freak?

BAILEY: That worry you, Tracker? That my wires may be loose? Someone you cannot reach?

TREVOR: I worry, Bailey, I am frightened, bewildered, terrified, urinating, excreting in my pants, that what makes you do what you do is because you are *too* human.

BAILEY: Pretty damn good for an intern.

TREVOR: "Something familiar?" "Knowing beyond what we know?"

(BAILEY smiles and nods.)

(FINCH taps on mirror/window and TREVOR summons Marlow, who enters and stands guard as TREVOR exits to Observation Room.)

FINCH: *(Looking at computer.)* This guy purchased five cell phones in March from a store in Wyoming. Each phone with one year's service paid in full in cash. He made one call the day he blew that first gas pump. Today three phones received calls when Rinehart called them . . . and the three stations blew.

TREVOR: Jesus.

FINCH: *(Shows computer to TREVOR.)* This guy's parents say that as a child he had a cell phone, but after age fourteen he refused to own or use a cell phone. Refused to use the Internet at home or school. Refused to have friends. None in college. None in law school. Who does that?

TREVOR: *(Stares at BAILEY through mirror/window.)* What teenage boy locks himself in solitary confinement? Practices drowning?

FINCH: No evidence of a cult, a gang, a fanatical religious group . . . I get chills. This guy went out of his way for us to catch him at the beginning.

TREVOR: This isn't the beginning. The beginning started at age fourteen.

FINCH: So, you're saying we caught him near the end.

TREVOR: I'm saying, you're hoping this is near the end.

FINCH: *(Pause, taken aback.)* Well, at least he likes talking with you, Trevor. Even if he is a monster.

TREVOR: Monsters we could stop.
(Pause.)
Do you have an Ipad?

FINCH: In my brief case.

(TREVOR opens FINCH'S brief case and pulls out a small purse. FINCH grabs purse and frowns.)

TREVOR: *(Pulls out Ipad.)* I'm going on a Google expedition. *(Enters Interrogation Room.)*

FINCH: *(Calls after TREVOR.)* You're welcome.
(Mumbles.)
Who doesn't own an Ipad?

TREVOR: While you were in self-exile, some nifty inventions moved civilization along.

BAILEY: I was surrounded by Ipads in classes, thank you.

TREVOR: Google?

BAILEY: Classmates crammed Google down my throat. How many miles ice-hockey players skate in a match, which countries say "elevator" and which say,
(British accent.)
"lift."

TREVOR: *(Types on Ipad.)* Let's look up . . . uh . . . "Time bomb explosives." That's what's next? Right? Timers?

BAILEY: It's your imaginative journey.

(MARLOW points to sign stating, "No Electronics.")

TREVOR: Wow.
(Shows Ipad to MARLOW.)
A list of terrorist explosions with timers. Hm.
(Shows Ipad to BAILEY.)
Here are the names of the terrorists. Guess you'll be next on this list. Let's look at your colleagues' names and motives, shall we?

BAILEY: They are not my colleagues.

TREVOR: I bet they all said that. "I'm unique" . . . Here we go. 2006. Moscow market bombing, racially motivated. Thirteen killed, forty-six injured. And . . . 1998. Omagh bombing. Northern Ireland. Anti-British campaign. Twenty-nine killed. 220 injured. And . . . Pan Am Flight, Korean Air flight. Oh! 1977, Lucona sinking in Indian Ocean. Six dead. Look! That was for insurance fraud.

BAILEY: Not my colleagues.

TREVOR: Bet you're dying to know who was first . . . 1871. Attack on the Mosel. That's a ship. Eighty dead. Yep, also insurance fraud. Alexander Keith. Wonder what they will list beside your name? "Health care activist?"

BAILEY: Isn't your work day over?

TREVOR: *(Looks at watch.)* By golly, you're right. Even without that clock. Well, time to go live life. Meanwhile, enjoy that solitude you rehearsed for. Sergeant? Please escort him to his cell, but do not, I repeat, do not converse with him.

MARLOW: Yes sir.

TREVOR: *(Walks toward Observation Room but then pauses.)* Oh, and during transport? At all times, hood him. *(Stares at BAILEY.)* Standard procedure for HVTs, isn't that right, Bailey?

(BAILEY sneers at TREVOR and then MARLOW hoods him while TREVOR exits.)

(Lights to black.)

Act One · Scene Two

TREVOR and TEANNA'S living room. Late afternoon. TREVOR is sitting on the couch, preoccupied looking over his notes.

TEANNA enters, listening to music on her head phones. She is humming, singing, and dancing to a favorite tune. Eventually, she sits next to TEVOR and quietly opens and reads an invitation. She sets the invitation on the coffee table and sings again. She becomes frustrated that TREVOR does not pay attention and snatches away his notebook.

TREVOR: Wait! I'm studying.

(TEANNA stands and begins singing and pulling on TREVOR'S arms to stand.)

TREVOR: No, no, no.

TEANNA: Yes, yes, yes.

TREVOR: I can't hear the music.

TEANNA: *(Removes her earphones.)* In your head.
(She pulls TREVOR to his feet to dance and leads him in dancing, twirling him around while singing. They laugh and TEANNA sings some of the lyrics in baby talk. They collapse onto the couch, hugging and laughing.)

TREVOR: Oh my gosh. You are something else, woman.

TEANNA: *(Slides to prone position on back. Pulls TREVOR so he is on all fours kneeling above her. Seductively.)* Does Trevor want to drive Teanna out to her grandparents' little farm?

TREVOR: It'd be awfully dark by the time we can got there. Who knows what that may lead to?

TEANNA: Yesssss. And if we hurry we can catch the sunset. Remember the last time how we watched that old sun set?

TREVOR: *(Laughs.)* I do remember.
(Quiet.)
How it started.
(Slowly, passionately kisses TEANNA on lips.)
How it ended.
(Gently rubs TEANNA'S pregnant abdomen.)

TEANNA: *(Puts her hand over Trevor's hand as they both gently rub her abdomen. Pulls Trevor to be over her again. Baby talk voice.)* So will Tracker drive his little Kiwi out to the farm?

TREVOR: *(Baby talk voice.)* Tracker wants to drive his little Kiwi upstairs . . . Now.

TEANNA: *(Baby talk.)* Oh my. What's a good Christian girl to do?

TREVOR: I think Teanna remembers very clearly what to do.

TEANNA: *(Baby talk.)* Are you gonna put on your big black bowtie for Teanna?

TREVOR: Bowtie?
(Moves to a sitting position.)
What bowtie?

TEANNA: *(Sits up.)* When you danced like a Chippendale?

TREVOR: *(Embarrassed.)* Danced like a Chippendale? . . . Oh! Big black . . . Yes.

TEANNA: You were one drunk skunk, Agent Tracker Wolf.

TREVOR: I was drunk. I don't even . . . Hey? Where did I get that bowtie?

TEANNA: I gave it to you. A preview of some amazing future gift.

TREVOR: Gift?

TEANNA: *(Teasing.)* Uh huh. But Teanna isn't telling.

TREVOR: My birthday?

TEANNA: *(Teasing.)* Nooooo.

TREVOR: Not my birthday? Hm. Not my birthday. Uh . . .

TEANNA: Maybe some kind of anniversary?

TREVOR: Anniversary? Oh anniversary. Yes. We do have, uh huh.

TEANNA: *(Still silly.)* Hint. That big black bowtie would be even more *awesome* . . . if I put you in a tuxedo.

TREVOR: *(Puzzled.)* Put me in a tuxedo?
(Aware.)
You're putting me in a penguin suit?

TEANNA: *(Shows invitation to Trevor.)* The hospital fund raiser.

TREVOR: Oh no, no, no. No tuxedo.

TEANNA: One little time a year.
(Makes pleadingly sad face.)

TREVOR: There's no way it's been a year . . . July. Oh shit. Tea? Do I really have to?

TEANNA: All of Mommy and Daddy's friends will be there.

TREVOR: Your parents live in New Zealand. They won't know if we dress up for a fund raiser or go bowling.
(Sexually.)
Or something else.

TEANNA: Gladys Rinquist?

TREVOR: *(Sighs.)* Gladys.

TEANNA: *(Stands and puts on Trevor's FBI baseball-style hat.)* Let's march upstairs, Agent Trevor Wolf.

TREVOR: Ohhhhh . . . Okay Mrs. Teanna Wolf. For you? I'll rub elbows with the "old money."

TEANNA: "Stuffy old money." But my you clean up well. Especially when I dress you. But for now, I am going to undress you. *And* . . . pull on your big bowtie.
(Places hat on TREVOR'S head.)

TREVOR: My bowtie is getting bigger by the second.

TEANNA: *(Yells as exits upstairs.)* Then you better hurry!

TREVOR: *(Laughs, walks to stairs, pausing to pull off FBI hat and examine it a moment. Hangs hat on coat rack. Yells upstairs.)* Did you know there's a town named Tuxedo?

TEANNA: One . . . two . . . three . . .

TREVOR: Okay, I'm coming.
(Exits as runs upstairs.)

(Lights to black.)

Act One · Scene Three

Interrogation Room. Morning. TREVOR is sitting reading papers. MARLOW guides BAILEY to a seat in the Interrogation Room, leaving BAILEY hooded.

TREVOR: *(Talks as continues to look at papers.)* Thank you. You can leave us now.

(MARLOW exits.)

TREVOR: Your parents should be back in the states tomorrow. Someone on our team will interro . . . question them.

BAILEY: *(Mumbles.)* Not you?

TREVOR: Pardon me?

BAILEY: *(Louder.)* Not you?

TREVOR: No. Did you sleep well last night?

BAILEY: *(Shrugs as mumbles.)* Guess so.

TREVOR: I cannot understand you when you talk down into the table like that.
(Removes BAILEY'S hood.)

(BAILEY looks at Trevor. He has a cut on his face, a black eye, and his face is pale and sweaty.)

TREVOR: What in the hell?
(Rapidly walks to door and yells.)
What in the hell happened?

MARLOW: *(Enters.)* Sir?

TREVOR: What the fuck happened to Bailey's face?

(MARLOW shrugs.)

TREVOR: I asked you a question.

MARLOW: I just came on duty, sir. He was already in his hood, sir.

TREVOR: Bailey?

(BAILEY shrugs.)

TREVOR: *(Closely examines BAILEY'S face.)* Shit.
(To Marlow.)
Stay with him while I get to the bottom of this.
(Exits to Observation Room.)
Fuck. Where is everyone?
(Calls on mobile.)
Finch? What the fuck happened to Bailey? . . . I don't want to wait until you get here I . . . oh.

FINCH: *(Enters talking on mobile and carrying brief case.)* Let me get settled.

TREVOR: Look at him!
(Points at Bailey through mirror/window.)
He has cuts on his face, a black eye, and looks like he was placed on the rack.

FINCH: No one has authority to approach this guy but you and me. And Martin and Bledsoe.

TREVOR: "And Martin and Bledsoe?" You're shittin' me. I agreed to interrogate Bailey if only I deal with him. Martin and Bledsoe get hard-ons fantasizing about sending people back to the Inquisition.

FINCH: They are effective with some very difficult detainees.

TREVOR: No! They are not! They boast they are "effective." They only "acquire" intel they already dreamed up was going to be intel. Read their reports. They never get the truth.

FINCH: I'll talk with them.

TREVOR: What am I supposed to do? Turn my back for a few hours? Do like Martin and Bledsoe boast they tell agents overseas to do? "Turn a blind eye?" Those ruffians only read the X-rated portions of the KUBARK Manual.

FINCH: *You* are invested in this case, Trevor, but do not, I repeat, do not refer to higher-ranking agents pejoratively. Not in my place of work. Not in my presence. Do we have an understanding?

TREVOR: Martin and Bledsoe are exactly what Bailey wants. He welcomes torture.

FINCH: Are you hearing me?

TREVOR: *(Pauses and composes self.)* I hear you.

FINCH: And you understand what I am saying?

TREVOR: I understand.

FINCH: Good. Now I'll talk with those two . . . higher-ranking agents. I feel confident we will come to an understanding. Now patch up any damage you think was done.

TREVOR: *(Mumbles.)* I *think* was done?

FINCH: Tracker!

TREVOR: *(Sighs.)* Yes ma'am.

(Enters Interrogation Room and moves his chair close to BAILEY, sits.)

TREVOR: I'm sorry Bailey. It won't happen again. I promise. *(Stands. To MARLOW.)*
Uncuff him.

FINCH: *(Starts to knock on mirror/window but retracts.)*

MARLOW: Sir?

TREVOR: From now on. when I'm with Bailey in this room? He will be uncuffed. Understood?

MARLOW: *(Looks at mirror/window, then at TREVOR, then at mirror/window again, then at TREVOR.)* Yes sir.
(Unlocks BAILEY'S cuffs, but leaves BAILEY in shackles.)

TREVOR: And get this table out of here, too.

MARLOW: Yes sir.
(Folds table and carries it as exits.)

(TREVOR remains standing, thinking to self.)

(BAILEY grins to self and stretches.)

(Lights to black.)

Act One · Scene Four

Living room of TREVOR and TEANNA'S home. Early Evening. TREVOR is lying on couch, reading and drinking water with his back to TEANNA, who is wrapping a gift as she talks.

TEANNA: So, this five-year-old girl? Not the one with cystic fibrosis but the other five-year-old girl? . . . Are you listening?

TREVOR: *(Looks up.)* The one with kidney infection.

TEANNA: Severe kidney infection. She should stay in the hospital, but she doesn't have health insurance. So, the chairman of pediatrics ordered her to be treated as an outpatient. Are you getting this?

TREVOR: That would be bad for her.

TEANNA: "Bad?" Probably *fatal.*

TREVOR: Fatal.

TEANNA: So, I argued with her, my chairman Natalie. Remember Natalie?

TREVOR: Small streak of purple in her hair.

TEANNA: Purple streak? That was Natalie the receptionist. My chairman does not have a streak of purple or any other color of hair. I promise. You met Natalie, Dr. Zell, at our Halloween party. Anyway. Natalie said talk to the infectious disease team and their coordinators. So, I did. The girl was discharged tonight. She'll die. While I was living in New Zealand with Mommy and Daddy, medical care was a God-given right. Are you sure you're listening?

TREVOR: I don't want to talk about dying children. I'm sorry. I don't.

TEANNA: Okay. Tell me about your day.

TREVOR: Tea. I can't. You know I can't.

TEANNA: Well then, I can't either.
(Resumes wrapping gift.)
That's what I get for marrying a "secret agent" . . . Cindy and Kaitlyn are heaps jealous I sleep with an exciting, mysterious guy.
(Kisses Trevor on top of head.)
They ask about you, but I don't answer them. Oh! Did you try to buy gas today? The stations are all closed. Because of that stupid bomb in Montana.

TREVOR: Florida, South Carolina, Wyoming.

TEANNA: Wyoming. Close to Montana. I was supposed to ride with Angela tomorrow for her one-month well-baby check. *(Pauses.)*

TREVOR: But?

TEANNA: Angela's car is empty and I wasn't about to tell her I have a wee bit of gas in my car that I want to save in case I have complications.

TREVOR: You have five more months, Tea.

TEANNA: I could have complications. I'm a pediatrician. Anything could happen.

TREVOR: Uh huh.

TEANNA: *(Sternly.)* Tracker? I could.

TREVOR: Okay. You could. It's a good thing you are saving gas for emergencies.

TEANNA: You don't think I'm being selfish?

TREVOR: I think . . . I think . . . you are being . . . cautious. Properly, thoughtfully, realistically cautious.

TEANNA: I feel a tiny bit selfish.

TREVOR: You are just looking out for our future.

TEANNA: Angela would do the same if she were in my shoes.

TREVOR: I'm sure she would.

TEANNA: But then, I would think she was being bloody selfish.

TREVOR: Teanna! You are doing the right thing.

TEANNA: If you say so, Tracker, but if you don't think I am, I'll call Angela and tell her I'll drive her. Use up my last bit of gas.

TREVOR: You should not drive Angela tomorrow. In fact, I forbid it.

TEANNA: *(Completes bow on gift.)* There. That looks lovely.

(Sound of mobile ringing.)

TREVOR: *(Answers.)* Hello . . . seven?
(Excited.)
All right! Get his ass down to the interrogation room. I don't want anyone talking to him before I get there.
(Ends call.)
Can I use your car? Mine's on "E."

(TEANNA sighs, then drags feet as walks to purse and gets car keys. Dangles keys over her head, holds them behind

her back, and then runs away, playfully playing "keep away.")

TREVOR: *(Chases TEANNA, jumping over couch to get to her. Finally yells to her as he pats his own belly to signal her to be careful about the baby.)* Whoa, whoa, easy. The baby.

TEANNA: *(Stops.)* The baby's fine.

(TREVOR walks to TEANNA slowly, kisses her, and suddenly grabs the keys and laughs as he walks away.)

TEANNA: You win.

TREVOR: Yes, I did.
(Gathers belongings.)
Thanks, Tea.
(Walks toward door.)

TEANNA: Bye.

TREVOR: *(Pauses.)* I love you.

TEANNA: I love you, too . . . Jerk.

(TREVOR laughs and exits.)

TEANNA: *(Calls on house phone.)* Angela? . . . Hi. It's Tea . . . Good, good. Listen. Sorry but Tracker just ran off with my car for "some big secret" agent mission . . . I don't know, but I'm sure he'll use up my last bit of gas. There's nothing I could do. You don't hate me, do you?

(Lights to black.)

Act One · Scene Five

Interrogation Room. Evening. The room no longer has a table, just two chairs. BAILEY is sitting on a bench with handcuffs and hood as MARLOW quietly stands over him. TREVOR is in the Observation Room, looking at the computer. He becomes excited over a discovery.

TREVOR: *(Talks as he enters Interrogation Room.)* Guess what we found? No. Better Bailey? You tell me what we found.

(MARLOW removes BAILEY'S hood and hand cuffs.)

BAILEY: *(Meditates with eyes closed and taking deep breaths.)* What time is it?

TREVOR: 9:33 pm.

BAILEY: You interrupted my meditation.

TREVOR: You will have enormous amounts of time for meditation.

BAILEY: I'm sorry, Tracker.

TREVOR: For?

BAILEY: Whatever it is they found that interrupted your dinner, your family time.

TREVOR: Receipts for cell phone purchases.
(Dangles group of stapled receipts.)

BAILEY: *(Opens eyes.)* Fourteen cell phones?

TREVOR: *(Pause.)* Seven. Seven additional cell phone purchases.

BAILEY: Seven? Oops. Must have miscounted.
(Resumes meditating.)

TREVOR: Fourteen?
(Pause.)
Look at me Bailey. Fourteen?

(BAILEY opens eyes and nods.)

TREVOR: Shit . . . We physically found one cell phone attached to a detonator and C4 at a BP station near Scottsdale, Arizona.

BAILEY: Since the Gulf Oil Spill, everyone hates BP. You oughta let it blow.

TREVOR: That phone had been called twice from another cell phone, a pre-paid phone sold to a Mr. Buck T. Jetson.

BAILEY: Jetson? Like the space-family cartoon.

TREVOR: That Jetson phone was used to call seven other prepaid phones.
(Examines receipts, turning page for each name.)
The other phones were bought by Ace Bruce Wayne, Clark McKent, Yogi LeBera, Booboo Smith, and Robin Hood, Arthur Hood, and Merlin Hood.

BAILEY: The next group of seven has better names.

TREVOR: And guess what we, no, you tell me what we found on the Booboo Smith phone at the Scottsdale BP station.

BAILEY: Uh . . . The alarm was set?

(TREVOR nods.)

BAILEY: So, from 1:20 this afternoon until 9:30 tonight, all the US bomb squads put together found one Booboo Smith phone?

TREVOR: We are tracking them by pin-pointing their relationships to cell towers.

BAILEY: How is that working for you?

TREVOR: That particular small phone company has software "glitches."

(FINCH enters Observation Room, tired and disheveled. She notices Trevor and Bailey and observes.)

BAILEY: Imagine that. You could call the cell phones. You'd learn their locations instantly.
(Makes explosion sound.)
Or wait for the alarms to go off.
(Makes explosion sound.)

TREVOR: *(Calls on his mobile.)* Hey, it's me. When was that alarm set for? . . . Thanks.

BAILEY: I thought you weren't allowed to have "electronics" in here.

MARLOW: *(Mumbles.)* He's not.

BAILEY: You could have just asked me. July 4th. Independence Day.
(Hums 1812 Overture and makes explosive sounds with gestures when the canons would boom in the music. He stands as he sings the last strains.)

(TREVOR points to MARLOW to seat BAILEY.)

MARLOW: Sit.

(MARLOW guides BAILEY to sitting back on bench and threatens him with handcuffs.)

TREVOR: Bailey? You're a child with money and dangerous toys. Didn't your parents ever spank you?

BAILEY: I was a model child. Tidy, punctual.

TREVOR: If I had been your father—

BAILEY: You would beat my ass? That's how a Redskin does it?

TREVOR: We wouldn't have needed to beat your ass, because . . . because we would have loved you Bailey . . . That's what my family did for me. What *we* would have done for you.

BAILEY: Are we finished here?

TREVOR: Are we?

BAILEY: I have to urinate . . . That means "piss."

TREVOR: Here's a yellow pad . . . and your "coloring crayon." *(Holds up a crayon.)*

(BAILEY frowns.)

TREVOR: What's wrong? You want a different color? *(Hands BAILEY a different crayon.)*

BAILEY: I said, I have to piss.

TREVOR: List where all fourteen phones are located. Enjoy your meditation.
(To MARLOW.)
I'm out of here.

BAILEY: I'm going to piss on myself.

TREVOR: Bailey's got homework to do. See that he does it. Then he can piss. If he still needs to.

MARLOW: Yes sir.

BAILEY: *(Yells to ceiling mic.)* I'm about to explode.

TREVOR: *(Yells to ceiling mic.)* We can get you another jump suit!
(Exits into Observation Room.)

(FINCH and TREVOR silently mouth ad lib lines such as, "You cannot break protocol and disallow toilet privileges," "He's just using that as an excuse," "What would the press say if they got hold of this?" "I don't care what the press would say," etc. They have much body language showing disagreement.)

(MARLOW silently gestures and mouths to BAILEY: "Do you need to go to the toilet?" BAILEY shakes head "no." MARLOW returns to usual spot and stands at parade rest.)

(Lights fade in Interrogation Room, remaining bright in Observation Room as FINCH and TREVOR argue in silence.)

(Lights to black.)

Act One - Scene Six

TREVOR'S living room. Early morning hours with nighttime lighting, no lamps on. TREVOR is sitting on couch in track pants with no shirt. TEANNA enters and sees TREVOR sitting in dark. She turns on a lamp and gets a blanket from the closet. She places the blanket over TREVOR'S shoulders and sits next to him.

TEANNA: Three-thirty. The bed felt cold . . . Care to talk about it?

TREVOR: Life will never return to normal.

TEANNA: Probably what your Native-American ancestors once said, right?

TREVOR: We Cheyenne . . . We survived. Sand Creek Massacre, Battle of Platte Bridge, Washita River. Fort Robinson Tragedy . . . Nothing normal lasts.

TEANNA: *(Grabs TREVOR'S hand.)* We'll last.

TREVOR: Yeah. Yeah we will.

TEANNA: What do you know?

(TREVOR shakes head.)

TEANNA: It's the Shell Bomber, isn't it?

TREVOR: One man. One young man.

TEANNA: He's getting to you.

TREVOR: People hug their children
  (Rubs TEANNA'S pregnant belly.)

Tell'em they love them. Guard who they'll hang out with, not hang out with. Select which TV shows, which video games.

TEANNA: Not even you have control, Trevor. Not even as the world's most amazing forensic criminologist.

TREVOR: When I'm in the same building as this guy? I don't feel safe going to the toilet. Feels like I should examine it before I piss.

TEANNA: I do that anyway.

TREVOR: Not for shit on the seat. So, I don't blow up.

TEANNA: Let's go to my grandparents' farm this weekend. Shuck some corn. Repair that leaky gutter by the porch swing.

TREVOR: When I sit in that swing, I like the gutter spout spraying on me. Takes me back.

TEANNA: What everyone else wants to repair, you treasure as is. I love that about you. Of course, that doesn't repair my great grandmother's antique cradle.

TREVOR: That cradle will be finished before our baby arrives. My pledge.

TEANNA: So? The farm?

TREVOR: We don't have gas to go that far.

(TEANNA looks disappointed.)

TREVOR: We can find something else to occupy our time.

TEANNA: *(Kisses TREVOR passionately.)* How's that for occupying time?

TREVOR: Show me again.
(Another passionate kiss.)
I think you're onto how people make it through wars.

TEANNA: Lots of babies are made during wars.

TREVOR: *(Kiss again and then in the middle of the kiss pulls away.)* That's it!

TEANNA: What's it?

TREVOR: What if you lose that special other person to war?

TEANNA: We aren't losing each other, Trevor. We're losing gasoline convenience.

TREVOR: No, no. This guy. He loves to act like he's a total loner. At war.

TEANNA: I detest sharing my home with these scumbags. Leave him at work, Trevor.

TREVOR: Maybe he lost someone.

TEANNA: Maybe this guy happens to be a monster.

TREVOR: That's what he wants me to think.

TEANNA: Not everyone is a teddy bear inside, Trevor.

TREVOR: He's a law student.

TEANNA: Precisely.

TREVOR: *(Stands and starts putting on shirt.)* He toys with me.
(Grabs car keys.)
He wants me to play his games.

TEANNA: Assure me, Tracker, you won't run back down there at four a.m.

TREVOR: No, no, I won't.
(Puts down keys.)
I won't Tea
(Sits, preoccupied.)

TEANNA: Your heart doesn't sound like it's into our wrapping ourselves around each other and listening to our child's heartbeat.

(TREVOR remains preoccupied.)

TEANNA: Oh Christ. You need sleep, Trevor. You know you do. Look at you.

TREVOR: Yeah. I suppose.

TEANNA: I want my husband to be my playmate. Is that so wrong?

TREVOR: I'll find gas for us for this weekend. We'll go to the farm. I swear on it.

TEANNA: *(Stands.)* Go play with your monster buddy. You'll be playing with him in your head the rest of the night whether you're here or at "the facility."

(TREVOR looks sad.)

TEANNA: No. No puppy eyes. Leave. Don't worry about me lying alone in a cold bed.

TREVOR: I do feel bad, Tea. I'll make it up to you. I promise.
(Smiles.)

TEANNA: Why don't you go fuck him?

(TEANNA walks up first few steps.)

TREVOR: Don't be like that, Tea.

TEANNA: *(Stops.)* I'm like that? Who's making me like that? I'm a pediatrician for Christ's sake, but do I abandon you day after day? Mr. FBI intern of the year. You know? Forget you. To hell with you and all of your bureau. *(Exits upstairs.)*

TREVOR: *(To self.)* And why am I like this? This? *(Takes FBI hat from rack. Talks softly to self.)* 'Cause I'm gonna make this shit stop. I'm gonna make this home, right here, safe for the three of us. *(Yells upstairs.)* My promise to you. My promise to our little girl. *(Throws FBI hat against wall.)*

(Lights to black.)

Act One · Scene Seven

Observation Room. Early morning. TREVOR is sitting and checking computer screen. He yawns. BAILEY and MARLOW enter the Interrogation Room. MARLOW removes BAILEY'S hood and hand cuffs and then yawns.

TREVOR: *(Immediately enters Interrogation Room with two cups of coffee, immediately speaking. Calm.)* Age fourteen, you declared war. Who left you? Died? Broke your heart? *(Hands coffee to BAILEY.)*

BAILEY: *(Smells coffee, delighted. Positions self to look at TREVOR'S watch.)* 5:15 a.m. Too early for donuts?

(TREVOR nods.)

BAILEY: Bagels? Soap?

(TREVOR shakes head.)

BAILEY: Find any of the cell phones?

TREVOR: Five.
(Holds up cell phone print out.)
Three from one set, two from the other set.

BAILEY: Here's where you can find five more.
(Hands yellow pad to TREVOR.)
Four remaining, if I did my arithmetic properly.

TREVOR: *(Looks at pad and compares his list with BAILEY'S list.)* We already found *three* of these on our own. This helps us to find only two more. That leaves *seven* we still need!

(BAILEY shrugs.)

TREVOR: *(Imitates shrug.)* What's this mean?

BAILEY: Not sure I know where the other seven are.

TREVOR: Did you have help?
(Pauses and speaks slowly as yells.)
Did you have help? . . . Accomplices?

BAILEY: I have memory lapses, Tracker. For real.

TREVOR: Too bad I don't have time to play games with you. Lives are on the line. But then you know all about that Bailey. You learned about that when you were fourteen.

BAILEY: When people play games, lives are always on the line. But dog gone it. People have this way of ignoring that little detail.

TREVOR: Who?

BAILEY: Lives on the line? Grandmothers, grandsons, brothers, cousins, aunts, neighbors.

TREVOR: Who?

BAILEY: Teachers, the milkman, your wife.

(TREVOR is taken aback.)

BAILEY: You forgot to remove your wedding ring this morning before you came to play with me . . . *Trevor.*

TREVOR: *(Taken aback again, pauses, then ignores that BAILEY knows his name.)* Who?

(BAILEY shakes head.)

TREVOR: Leukemia . . . Age thirteen . . . Medications, radiation. Best care money could buy. Seven years with a clean bill of health.

(Sound of phone beeping for text messages. MARLOW points at sign on wall stating, "No electronics.")

TREVOR: *(Looks at phone for text message.)* Two more phones found.
(Looks at list and compares to numbers on phone.)
Phones not on your list. I bet by this time tomorrow, Bailey, we have those last five.

BAILEY: Maybe I'll be able to remember.

TREVOR: I'm not here to make a trade.

BAILEY: *(Yells to ceiling mic.)* I have a piece of health care legislation I want Congress to pass and our President to sign.

TREVOR: You're kidding.

BAILEY: Now Tracker, Trevor. Did you lie about your reports going "high?" I need *high*.

TREVOR: Not even Congress can get Congress to pass a bill.

BAILEY: Reason I lit a fire beneath them, so to speak.

TREVOR: Okay. Let's say I bump your "legislation" up the ladder.

BAILEY: Sounds like a trade.

(FINCH enters Observation Room while listening to earphone music. Unpacks.)

TREVOR: What do I get? Names, locations of people helping you?

BAILEY: Have you seen evidence I am not acting alone?

TREVOR: Names, Bailey.

BAILEY: How about instead, I obtain adequate health care for your newborn baby? Soon to be newborn.

TREVOR: *(Stands.)* Cuff his ass!
(Exits to Observation Room.)

(MARLOW cuffs BAILEY and sits him in chair under interrogation lamp.)

(Lights fade so that the interrogation lamp is the only light in the Interrogation Room.)

FINCH: *(Is still unpacking brief case to start day.)* You got an early start.

TREVOR: I'm gonna fuckin' kill him!

FINCH: Need a donut?

TREVOR: How the fuck does Bailey know my name? How the fuck does he know that Teanna is expecting?

FINCH: This guy knows *what?*

TREVOR: I was this close to snapping his wind pipe.

FINCH: *(Calls on phone.)* Rinehart? Find out who has talked with Mr. Ross. Every possibility! Clear?
(Ends call.)
Damn Federal System. Sorry, Tracker.

(FINCH and TREVOR stare at BAILEY.)

TREVOR: "Something feels familiar." "Something feels familiar."
(Pauses.)
Do you remember that group of law students who toured through here six months ago?

(BAILEY sits motionless with constant shit-eating grin.)

FINCH: Sure.

TREVOR: Do you think . . . Shit. Do we have the list?

(FINCH nods and then she and TREVOR stare unflinchingly at BAILEY.)

(The Observation Room lights fade to blue with a hint of white light, while the full interrogation lamp brightly shines directly down on BAILEY in the Interrogation Room. Then lights in the Observation Room fade to black as the solitary interrogation lamp remains on BAILEY.)

(Lights to black.)

(INTERMISSION.)

Act Two · Scene One

TREVOR'S living room. Early evening. There are remnants of a July 4th meal with blue plates, red napkins, fresh flowers, and a partial candle all on the floor. Sound of video games.

TREVOR and TEANNA are sitting on the couch playing a video game. TREVOR is wearing a chef's apron and hat. They ad lib video game talk: "You cheat." "No, don't shoot me," etc.)

Sound of mobile ringing.

TREVOR turns off TV with remote and the video sounds end.

TEANNA: I was winning.

TREVOR: *(Laughs and answers mobile.)* Yeah . . . Okay . . . Good . . . Good. That's it then?
(Downbeat.)
Oh.
(Moves from couch to chair. Listens a long moment.)
Well, thanks for updating me.
(Ends call.)
The last two phones we didn't find blew up. Five p.m. No injuries.

TEANNA: Thank God for that. So, people can buy gas again, right? Back to normal?

TREVOR: Normal?
(Collapses deeper into chair.)

TEANNA: What?

TREVOR: One of the cell phones at the bombsites belonged to Ryan Dvorsky. Six months ago, Ryan took a group of law students to lunch, our bomber included. During lunch, Ryan's phone went missing.

TEANNA: But it was just Ryan's private phone. Right?

TREVOR: *(Nods.)* On his phone were agency numbers, co-worker's numbers.
(Looks at TEANNA.)
Our number.

TEANNA: Ryan called me last month.

TREVOR: What did he say?

TEANNA: He asked for you.

TREVOR: What did he say? What did you say?

TEANNA: Oh . . . "Oh, hi Ryan. This is Teanna. Haven't seen you since last year's picnic." And Ryan asked how things were going and I told him our baby was on schedule and I asked how his father's cancer was doing. Then we were disconnected.

TREVOR: Son of a bitch.
(Stands and paces.)

TEANNA: Do you think . . . ?

TREVOR: Do you still want to go to the farm?

TEANNA: We don't have gas.

TREVOR: We have gas. Finch made sure we do. But . . .

TEANNA: . . . But what?

TREVOR: *(Sits by TEANNA.)* The person who called you last month was not Ryan. It was the Shell Bomber. He knows.
(Calls on mobile.)
I do need that escort . . . Ten minutes? Okay.
(Ends call.)

TEANNA: You're scaring me.

TREVOR: You have ten minutes.

TEANNA: Ten minutes for what? I promised Angela we'd . . . You are coming with me, right?

TREVOR: I'll meet you in a couple of days.

TEANNA: I want you to come with me now.

TREVOR: The escort will stay with you 24/7.

TEANNA: Escort?

TREVOR: Jonathan and Margaret. You'll have nothing to worry about.

TEANNA: Here's an ultimatum: You are coming with me.

TREVOR: You'll be fine. I'll be fine. The baby will be fine. Trust me, Tea.

(TEANNA becomes quiet.)

TREVOR: Say something.
(Pauses.)
Anything.

TEANNA: When I met you two years ago? You excited me. Tied my stomach in knots. I never knew what to expect . . . I outgrew those feelings.
(Walks toward steps to upstairs.)

TREVOR: Tea?
(Walks toward TEANNA.)
Teanna?

(TEANNA climbs a few stairs, pauses, turns to talk.)

(Sound of home phone ringing.)

TEANNA: *(Shakes head and waves him off with hands.)* Go ahead. Answer it.
(Exits.)

TREVOR: *(Answers phone.)* Hello . . . Hello . . . Is anyone there? . . . Three more? Three more what? . . . Hello.
(Ends call.)
Shit.
(Calls on mobile.)
Finch? I just got an anonymous phone call . . . He said, "three more" . . . I don't know . . . You sure he's in his cell? No phone at all, right? . . . I . . .
(Pauses, whispers so TEANNA cannot hear.)
I know our protocol damn it. I don't trust it's being followed.

(Sounds of car horn outside.)

TREVOR: Tea's escort's here. See you in an hour.
(Ends call and walks to bottom of stairs and yells.)
Tea? Escort's early . . . Hurry it up!

(Lights to black.)

Act Two - Scene Two

Observation Room. Evening. FINCH is checking computer.

TREVOR: *(Enters.)* Any leads on that call to my house?

FINCH: Pay phone. A rarity these days. Smithsonian basement. No fingerprints. We're checking security videos.

TREVOR: Won't be service stations.

FINCH: Government buildings?

TREVOR: Maybe restaurants like in France. Subways like Japan.

FINCH: Trains like Spain. Timers . . . This guy's not working alone. Maybe suicide bombers.

TREVOR: Non-suicide bombers. Easier to recruit.

FINCH: "What we have here children" . . . is social collapse.

TREVOR: And the walls come tumbling down.

FINCH: Jericho. Didn't know you were religious.

TREVOR: Reagan. Berlin Wall. Obama. Arab Spring. *(Plays with pen, watching it as he clicks it.)*

FINCH: *(Also quiet as watches pen before speaking.)* I hate waiting.

TREVOR: They never show "waiting" on cop shows.

FINCH: *(Long quiet pause.)* You remember that new woman, long red hair, computer programmer?

TREVOR: Don't tell Tea, but yeah, I definitely remember her.

FINCH: Name's Wynell. I asked her to look for web pages, URLs with Mr. Ross's name. Different languages. She found one. Portuguese. Created from an Internet cafe. Then Wynell's computer crashed. Before it crashed, it sent out a few codes. Shut down runway lights at four small municipal airports in Vermont.

TREVOR: "Outposts all over Vermont." "Little unimpressive municipal airports."

FINCH: What the hell are you talking about?

TREVOR: Bailey's flexing his muscles. Previews.
(Pause.)
Do you think he hacked our system?

FINCH: Any reason to think he did not?

TREVOR: I'm starting to hate this guy.

FINCH: I can pull you off this case.

TREVOR: I have it under control.

(Sound of office phone ringing.)

FINCH: *(Answers phone.)* Yes . . . Where? . . . Uh huh . . . Okay . . . Uh huh . . . Awful.
(Ends call, pauses.)
Car bombs. Three Walmart entrances. Texas, Kentucky, Oregon. Eleven dead. Twenty-six injured. The drivers calmly walked away.

TREVOR: Shit! Do we have the Walmart videos?

FINCH: Same exact pattern at all three. Vehicles were stolen ambulances. License plates had numbers and letters that make no sense. Drivers wore hoodies and batman masks.

TREVOR: All three?

FINCH: *(Nods.)* How does this loner find people to aid him?

TREVOR: Thousands of people occupied Wall Street, occupied major cities and small towns across the US. People are unhappy . . . Walmarts . . . "Colgate whitening toothpaste at Walmart." Was that a clue for me? Bailey's way to toy with me?

FINCH: You're not making sense.

TREVOR: Can you talk to Bailey while I grab my transcripts?

FINCH: I'm likely to rip out his intestines and feed them to him.

TREVOR: Shit. I was just going to shoot him in the kneecap. Can you pull the transcripts?

(Sound of office phone ringing.)

FINCH: *(Answers phone.)* Finch!
(Puts hand over phone to whisper to TREVOR.)
Homeland Security, Secretary Kelly.

TREVOR: Uh oh.

FINCH: *(To phone.)* Hi John . . . Yes sir . . . Yes sir, we would love to do that. In fact, we were just fantasizing about disemboweling him . . . He says he wants to improve health care . . . Insane but ahead of us . . . When? . . . Uh huh . . . Uh huh.

TREVOR: *(Whispers.)* What?

FINCH: *(Whispers to Trevor.)* Two Senators, two representatives, and the Secretary of Health and Human Services received this guy's health legislation in the mail.
(To phone.)
Pardon me. What was that? . . . Uh huh . . . We're on top of it. We'll keep you posted.
(Ends call.)
They want someone to review a copy of his legislative proposal with him.

TREVOR: I pity that poor bastard.

FINCH: Secretary Kelly and Secretary Price think his proposal was "ingenious."

TREVOR: Shit. We don't negotiate with terrorists. Never. That's in the manual!

FINCH: Our country is frozen up. Down on its knees.
(Looks at large document, pauses.)
Hope you're up to this.
(Hands document to TREVOR.)

TREVOR: Me? Shit! Does Secretary Kelly know you have an intern leading this interrogation?

FINCH: He will if you earn a failing grade.

TREVOR: No pressure. Don't worry about me. I'm fine.

FINCH: This guy trusts you. I've watched everyone else around here interrogate. Ain't no way this guy would tell them half what he tells you.
(Exits.)

TREVOR: *(Looks at papers and then yells after FINCH.)* Hell of a class, Finch.

(Lights to black.)

Act Two · Scene Three

Interrogation Room. BAILEY is pacing, impatient while TREVOR is sitting and reading.

TREVOR: *(Finishes reading document, sarcastic.)* Clear ideas. Excellent sentence structure. Eloquent.

BAILEY: Thank you for your rip-roaring, enthusiastic critique.
(Sits.)
It's killing you to not ask about the car bombs, isn't it?

TREVOR: Car bombs?

BAILEY: Tracker? How can I trust you if you and I don't talk openly?

TREVOR: Openly? Okay.
(Passes yellow pad to BAILEY.)
Write down the names of three people who recently drove three stolen ambulances while wearing batman masks.

BAILEY: Shit!
(Laughs.)
Now you have to admit, that's funny.

TREVOR: Funny? Eleven people died. But then you didn't give a fuck when the first two people died.

BAILEY: Ahhhh, Tracker, come on now. I care . . . How many casualties were there in the past twenty-four hours?

TREVOR: Eleven.

BAILEY: Both sides of the war.

TREVOR: There's one side to this war, Bailey. Your side.

BAILEY: In the last twenty-four hours, how many people died because they were refused medical care? Not counting people who died living in cardboard boxes. Five? Twenty? Fifty? No. Two hundred people. Every day, Tracker. Two hundred people. Oh. What? You don't give a fuck about them, Tracker?

TREVOR: Two hundred plus the eleven you killed. By playing God, Bailey, you upped the number of dead people by eleven.

BAILEY: Where was God when . . .
(Becomes uncomfortable, breaks eye contact.)

TREVOR: *(Waits a moment.)* When what?

BAILEY: *(Shakes head.)* The bombings will stop. I'll make them stop.

TREVOR: You can do that?

BAILEY: We're entering the next stage.

TREVOR: Next stage?

BAILEY: The legislation. There must be a way we can assert stronger pressure on the President and Congress. We can do this, Tracker.

TREVOR: We? We Bailey? Oh, that's a new tactic, "Get interrogators to help terrorists be better terrorists."

BAILEY: Give me a positive idea, Tracker, something I haven't thought of.

TREVOR: Uh . . . Why not? . . . What about . . . Post a copy of your legislation in the *New York Times.* Let the public lean on our elected officials.

BAILEY: Wow! Great idea.

TREVOR: Don't patronize me, Bailey. You already thought of it. But here's the catch, what if the public fuckin' hates your legislation?

BAILEY: They will like it.

TREVOR: You sure of that? We, the collective majority have a history of making terrible choices and having to live with the terrible outcomes.

BAILEY: This is good legislation.

(TREVOR knocks on mirror/window and signals for FINCH to enter Interrogation Room. She enters and frowns at BAILEY.)

TREVOR: *(Hands document to FINCH.)* We need copies of "this-good-idea" legislation to go to the *New York Times*. *(Looks at BAILEY and gestures "more?")*

BAILEY: Oh, and *Time, The Washington Post,* and the *Wall Street Journal.*

(FINCH snatches document and exits.)

BAILEY: The newspapers have three days to print that story on their front pages, *Time Magazine* one week. Congress has twelve days to pass the legislation, the President an additional day to sign the legislation. If they fail, bombings resume the following day.

TREVOR: You believe Congress can move in twelve days?

BAILEY: I will give you the exact, and I do mean exact headline to accompany the health care legislation story. When my people see that—

TREVOR: "My people?" Wow! Now it's, "my people." You're a CEO of terrorists?

BAILEY: Listen to me.

TREVOR: All ears.

BAILEY: When my people see that exact wording, printed in an exact font I will give you, then there will be no more bombings. Any incorrect wording or incorrect fonts, and there will be unbelievable pandemonium.

TREVOR: Pandemonium.

BAILEY: You have my word.

TREVOR: I want your written, signed confession.

BAILEY: You want me as a casualty of this war, Tracker? I hoped you would admire my legislative skills. You will have my signed confession.

TREVOR: Everything seems on automatic pilot, Bailey. Legislation gets delivered on schedule to the proper people. Cars blow up, gas pumps blow up, Walmarts blow up, all on schedule. I'm sure "unbelievable pandemonium" will be on schedule. Even if you were dead, all of this would move forward on schedule.

BAILEY: Eight years of planning.

TREVOR: So, Bailey? Now are you listening?

BAILEY: "All ears."

TREVOR: Why? Why did you set it up to be caught on top of that North Carolina mountain? You begged those Watauga County Officers to take you.

BAILEY: *(Laughs.)* I did. At first the sheriff's deputy asked if I saw the person who parked the vehicle that blew up by the pumps. I answered, "Yes sir. He was my height, my weight, had my eye and hair color, wore clothes exactly like I am wearing now." I even added, "He was carrying a Panasonic video camera, just like my camera." The deputy laughed, "Shoot, you could be the suspect." It was really a challenge to get those rednecks to contact Homeland Security and issue an extra-ordinary rendition to get me transferred here.

TREVOR: Just "rendition," Bailey. Not "extraordinary." Just "rendition."

BAILEY: You sure?

TREVOR: Another the-cops-were-idiots story. Go ahead, laugh. But Bailey? Why did you want to be caught?

BAILEY: Maybe . . . Maybe I am smart. Maybe even with being smart and clever, I don't know the why. But it was a feeling, a feeling in my gut that I could only succeed if I did get caught, spent time here with you. You know how you get those feelings sometimes and you don't know why.

TREVOR: Who?

BAILEY: Who what?

TREVOR: Who?

BAILEY: Who what?

TREVOR: You launched your war at age fourteen. Leukemia. Age thirteen. Remission age fourteen.

BAILEY: I won't talk about my leukemia. Off limits.

TREVOR: I have your hospital records. Age thirteen. Six kids in your leukemia unit.

BAILEY: How long before Teanna delivers? Did you move her somewhere a bit safer?

TREVOR: *(Picks up file.)* Here are the names of the six from your unit: Jonathan Ross, same last name as you but no relation. Amy Brown, Jeremy Wilmuth, Alfonzo Ortiz, in parenthesis it says he went by "Mex."
(Stops reading.)
"Mex."
(Tosses down file.)

BAILEY: You said there were six names.

TREVOR: Something felt familiar. "Knowing beyond what we know." "Mex."

(BAILEY shakes his head, prompting TREVOR to walk to switches and turn off audio switch.)

BAILEY: What did you just do?

TREVOR: I turned off the audio to the recorder.

(FINCH knocks on mirror/window. TREVOR holds up his hand signally silence to FINCH'S knocking.)

TREVOR: So? Mex.

BAILEY: *(Pause.)* Mex and I entered the leukemia program the same day. A Saturday in March. I had money. Mex said he had God. He said, "God will see us both through." I didn't tell Mex, but I have never seen God. When you are rich, you don't need God. My father used to say that.

TREVOR: "Only the poor need God."

BAILEY: They have nothing else to fall back on.

TREVOR: Did Mex ever fall back on you or your parents' money?

BAILEY: You don't know my parents.

TREVOR: I'm starting to, Bailey, starting to. Did Mex ever fall back on you, not your parents, but on you?

BAILEY: Why do you act like you do?

TREVOR: How do I act?

BAILEY: You lie. Pretend to see. See who you are. See what you do. You take comfort in thinking that those lies help you excavate truth.

TREVOR: Excavate?

BAILEY: I'm not talking about truth or lies about whether you grew up with your grandfather in Wyoming, or you're a forensics intern studying under donut woman in there, or that you lie to your wife. I'm talking about essential, core "truth."

TREVOR: I don't know what you mean, "core truth."

BAILEY: No, you wouldn't.

TREVOR: What's your core truth, Bailey?

BAILEY: A moment here or there. A few minutes every afternoon in a not-so-nice hospital room. Several little moments like that, Tracker . . . Maybe they can last someone a lifetime. Maybe.

TREVOR: Moments with Mex.

BAILEY: I don't want to talk about Mex. I want to go back to my cell . . . Please, Tracker?

TREVOR: *(Pause.)* Can I tell you a story first?

BAILEY: I'd rather not.

TREVOR: About me, my story. All you have to do is listen.

BAILEY: If it makes you feel better.

(TREVOR pauses to look around room, then turns off all lights except overhead interrogation lamp. Moves to sitting on floor beneath lamp with legs crossed, "Indian style." Motions for BAILEY to join him. FINCH appears unhappy lights are off. Resumes working on computer. BAILEY looks around and then reluctantly sits beside TREVOR on floor.)

TREVOR: I told you that my grandfather gave me my nickname, Tracker. I was four. My grandfather taught me that everything the power of the world does is done in a circle. Moon orbits earth. Earth orbits sun. Four seasons cycle. The life of man is a circle from childhood to childhood. My grandfather lived long enough to join me in that circle.

BAILEY: Wise teacher.

TREVOR: I loved that "wise teacher." My sun and moon rose and set with that old man. I called him, Hawk. 'Cause he had a big nose. The night before my first day of kindergarten, which I refused to attend, Hawk sat me down, taught me that I had to earn the warrior energy and equilibrium of the elk. Elk has stamina and paces himself so he can run to the high country without fatigue, not fall prey. He said, elk's bugling would signal me of wolf's presence.

BAILEY: Wolf?

TREVOR: Wolf, in addition to being my last name, as you know from hacking our computers—

BAILEY: Sorry—

TREVOR: Wolf was Hawk's and my guardian, our animal spirit totem. Hawk said, wolf's mournful howls of loneliness guide us home. Hawk cautioned me. He said that I carry two wolves in my one heart. One wolf is angry, violent, vengeful. One wolf is compassionate, loving. Which wolf wins my heart depends upon which wolf I choose to feed.

BAILEY: I've heard that story. Somewhere. Somewhere familiar.
(Nods, pauses.)
Trevor? Why did Hawk nickname you, "Tracker?"

TREVOR: Hawk played hide and seek with me. I always found him. So . . . "Tracker." Hawk said one day he would appear to be gone, but if I kept my heart open, then I would forever be able to track him. Hawk "appeared gone" my freshman year of college.

BAILEY: Can you still track him?

TREVOR: Every day, every night, every sleep.

BAILEY: *(Pause.)* Tracker? . . . The reason Mex never fell back on me?

(TREVOR nods.)

BAILEY: Because . . . I was the one who fell back on Mex.

TREVOR: Mex.

BAILEY: *(Pause.)* Mex loved Madden. In the university hospital, Mex could play that video game forever. His favorite team was the Oakland Raiders. He taught me to use the QB vision.

TREVOR: Vision?

BAILEY: QB vision. A ray of light comes out of the quarterback's helmet. Helps you determine which receiver is open. Mex made me play as the 49ers.

TREVOR: The 49ers?

BAILEY: Yeah, 49ers suck, but Mex wanted me to be his rival. He beat me every time. Five, six hours a day, as many hours as Mex had the strength to play. We weren't two kids dying, put away in some leukemia unit. We were two teenagers rocking the sports world. Hit stick after hit stick. Mex hit me so hard my controller vibrated 'til my hands hurt. In those games, Mex was a winner.
(Nods, pauses.)
The hospital stopped his treatments. Mex didn't have money, so they . . . I got better. Mex got weaker. Our games got shorter. One day, I wheeled my chair down to Mex's room to finish the night-before's game. Another boy, Jared, was in Mex's bed. I wheeled room to room yelling for Mex. Janice, the nurse who always let Mex and me play a little longer, kneeled down beside me. She didn't speak and I didn't believe her silence. Janice handed me Mex's rosary beads. I threw them across the room. My mother sent Janice away. Mom was *jubilantly* happy to tell me that she and Dad were transferring me to a better hospital where they would be more comfortable around "their kind of people." They held me down, Tracker. They sedated me. In that black space and time, you know what? Mex was there. I felt him. I didn't ask to wake. I didn't want to wake . . . but I . . . I . . .

TREVOR: . . . woke.

77

(BAILEY, tearful, nods.)

TREVOR: And you declared war.

(BAILEY nods and TREVOR stands and turns on lights.)

BAILEY: Tracker? What would you have done?

TREVOR: *(Returns to Bailey.)* After losing my best friend?
(Kneels.)
Made a new friend.

BAILEY: You would. You would, Tracker. Now that I'm twenty-two, not fourteen, I would, too.

TREVOR: Yeah, you would.
(Summons MARLOW.)

BAILEY: Please don't write about Mex in your report.

(TREVOR nods and then uses Native American sign language to say, "Friend I understand." BAILEY nods and mirrors last gesture of TREVOR'S sign language.)

(MARLOW enters as TREVOR walks into Observation Room.)

FINCH: I reviewed the transcripts. It caught my eye that this guy told you about a Disneyland ride.

TREVOR: "The Matterhorn."

FINCH: I have teams searching Disneyland and Disneyworld rides.

TREVOR: Bailey imagined us riding to the top together. Two kid friends. I suppose two children would do that. They would reach the top . . . then die . . . not separate but together.

FINCH: Should we search other theme parks?

TREVOR: I'll ask Bailey.

FINCH: He'll tell you?

TREVOR: He will.
(Walks toward Interrogation Room.)

FINCH: Did you ever read *Crime and Punishment?*

(TREVOR stops and nods.)

FINCH: People, prisoners . . . They want to tell their stories. It drives them. Drives all of us . . . You are doing fine.

(TREVOR enters Interrogation Room and sits alone.)

(Lights to black.)

Act Two - Scene Four

TREVOR'S living room. Early afternoon. TREVOR is singing in broken words to music that he hears through headphones as he works on sanding an antique cradle. He does not notice TEANNA enter. He places a small gift in the cradle and covers it with a pink baby blanket.

TEANNA is wearing blue scrubs with significant blood spots. She finds TREVOR'S mobile phone on the mantle and carries it to him. She yanks out TREVOR'S earphones.

TREVOR: *(Startles.)* Hey!
(Looks at TEANNA'S face and scrubs.)
What the hell happened? You have blood all over you.

TEANNA: *(Hands mobile to Trevor.)* I've been calling you for five hours.

TREVOR: *(Turns on mobile and puts it into his pocket.)* My phone was off.

TEANNA: Natalie is dead.

TREVOR: What!

TEANNA: My boss Natalie. She's dead. Someone blew up our peds clinic.

TREVOR: What do you mean, "blew up?"

TEANNA: It's all over the news. Where were you?

TREVOR: Here. Are you okay?

TEANNA: No, I am not okay. My clinic blew up. Lucky for me I had walked over to the emergency department.

TREVOR: Jesus, Tea. I'm sorry.

TEANNA: You said this was over. Now things are blowing up again. You promised, Trevor.

TREVOR: It is over, Tea.

TEANNA: Three, Trevor! Three buildings!
(Turns on TV with remote.)

VOICE OF NEWS REPORTER: No official death count, but authorities expect the number of fatalities to be significant. One hospital in the Washington, DC area, one movie theatre in Tyler, Texas, and one McDonald's in Spokane, Washington. We now take you back to the studio where Senator—

(TEANNA mutes TV.)

TREVOR: Son of a bitch. Come here.
(Hugs Teanna.)

(Sound of mobile ringing.)

TREVOR: *(Ignores phone for a moment, but then speaks.)* Let it ring.

TEANNA: Answer it.

TREVOR: I'll call them back.

TEANNA: Answer it!
(Sits alone in chair.)

TREVOR: *(Answers mobile after looking to see who is calling.)* Yeah? . . . I had my phone off, okay? I'm on my way. *(Ends call.)*
You want me to call Angela to stay here with you?

TEANNA: I already called her.

TREVOR: Good. That's good.
(Prepares to leave, gets jacket from closet, sees TEANNA, and then walks to her and kneels.)
Tea, are you sure you're okay?

TEANNA: This? All of this? Is too much stress on the baby. I talked to Mom and Dad. They said we can stay with them.

TREVOR: In New Zealand? Jesus, Tea. How?

TEANNA: I told you when we had the baby, I wanted to be near Mom and Dad.

TREVOR: I work for the FBI in the US. That translates to what job in New Zealand?

TEANNA: Mom found me a position there as a pediatrician. We can live on my salary until you find something.

TREVOR: New Zealand? And you were going to talk about this when?

TEANNA: When are you not in crisis?

TREVOR: You can't go.

TEANNA: I what?

TREVOR: You heard me.

TEANNA: *(Whispers.)* Fuck you.
(Louder.)
I care about my child and obviously you do not.

TREVOR: Your child? Your child that you just made the decision to move to the other side of the fucking planet? What about my child, Tea?

TEANNA: Your child? If you care about having a child, or having a wife? You have a disgusting way of showing it.

(TREVOR is taken aback, shakes head, speechless, sits.)

TEANNA: One of us needs to make a grownup decision here, *Tracker.* Obviously, it is not going to be you. My mother and father bought both of us tickets. Either you come with us . . . or you do not come with us, Trevor. It's your choice.

(Lights to black.)

Act Two - Scene Five

Observation Room. Late afternoon. TREVOR is wearing a black suit and black shirt, reading reports.

FINCH: *(Enters.)* My you are dressed up today.

(TREVOR does not acknowledge the compliment.)

FINCH: Teanna okay?

TREVOR: She'll be fine.

FINCH: Good, good. That's a relief.

TREVOR: She's worried about the baby. She may spend time with her parents.

FINCH: Why don't you take some time off? Go with her. You earned it.

TREVOR: I see you found the amusement park bombs.

FINCH: Each and every one. Accurately where Mr. Ross told you they would be. Good job, Tracker.

TREVOR: As far as amusement parks are concerned.

FINCH: Yeah, well . . . Who could know? Thought you may want to see this.
(Hands papers to Trevor.)

TREVOR: *(Looks at papers.)* Bailey's leukemia relapsed?

FINCH: Six months ago. Even though his parents donated a full leukemia care unit to the hospital where he was treated, this strange man refused further treatment.

TREVOR: *Refused?* What is this? A suicide mission? So, all hope of a logical conclusion is shit?
(Despair.)
We've lost.

FINCH: I'm pulling you back. Bringing in Martin and Bledsoe.

TREVOR: *(Shakes head.)* I can do this.

FINCH: Your wife's clinic just blew up. It's personal now.

TREVOR: I can . . . Please.

FINCH: No.

TREVOR: Just give me a minute.
(Sits and pauses.)
Get me a coffee and a donut.

FINCH: Coffee and a donut?

TREVOR: Maple frosted.

FINCH: God almighty. I thought I was boss around here. Okay. But do not move out of that seat until I get back. Maple frosted.
(Exits.)

(Lights rise on Interrogation Room as door buzzes. MARLOW guides BAILEY in and to a chair. as BAILEY loudly hums a religious hymn.)

BAILEY: Thank you, Marlow.

MARLOW: Uh huh.
(Stands at parade rest at his usual spot.)

(TREVOR immediately sees MARLOW and BAILEY. He looks to see that FINCH is not close by. He enters Interrogation Room and paces with quiet agitation.)

(MARLOW disconnects handcuffs from waist belt and TREVOR quickly and silently motions for MARLOW to not remove hood and cuffs. TREVOR motions for MARLOW to leave and MARLOW exits.)

(TREVOR stands quietly but agitated near BAILEY. He takes off wedding ring and places it in jacket pocket. Takes off his jacket and places it on bench. Rolls up shirtsleeves.)

BAILEY: That you, Tracker?

(TREVOR agitatedly walks behind BAILEY, jerks BAILEY to his feet, kicks BAILEY'S knees out so that he falls to his knees. TREVOR smashes BAILEY'S face into the floor.)

BAILEY: *(Struggling to speak.)* Tracker?

(TREVOR pulls BAILEY back up and pulls off BAILEY'S hood. BAILEY'S nose is bloody.)

TREVOR: You seem surprised, Bailey. Think you can blow up children and old people in hospitals and movie theatres? *(Slams Bailey's face on floor, pulls BAILEY back up.)* I trusted you. I did everything you said, fucker. "Exact headlines." "Exact fonts." "Take it higher, higher!"

BAILEY: What are you talking about?

(TREVOR slams BAILEY'S face against the floor. BAILEY rolls onto his back. TREVOR sits on BAILEY'S chest with his knees pinning BAILEY'S arms. He pulls back his fist to hit BAILEY in face, but then pauses. He suddenly pulls gun out of holster and holds muzzle against BAILEY'S forehead.)

TREVOR: Here's your chance for that moment of core truth.

(MARLOW rushes in.)

(FINCH enters Observation Room, sees situation and quickly picks up phone and talks quickly with distress.)

MARLOW: Sir? Put the gun away, sir.

TREVOR: *(Briefly points gun at MARLOW and then back at BAILEY.)* I'm a little busy here, Marlow.

MARLOW: Sir? . . . Please. Not like this.

(FINCH mouths word, "wait" and gestures to self, "hold it.")

(TREVOR holds for a short pause, then screams as he jams barrel of gun into floor beside BAILEY'S head. Abruptly walks to bench and sits. Places gun beside him on bench.)

(MARLOW helps BAILEY to get off floor and to sit in chair. Checks BAILEY. Stands between TREVOR and BAILEY.)

MARLOW: *(To Trevor.)* You okay, sir?

TREVOR: I'm fine. We'll both be fine.

(FINCH mouths, "It's okay now." Hangs up phone, sits, and collects self.)

MARLOW: I think I should take the detainee back to his cell, sir.

(TREVOR shoots a dirty look at MARLOW. MARLOW pauses, looks at both TREVOR and BAILEY. BAILEY gestures, "It's okay." MARLOW lifts gun from bench, pointing it at floor.)

MARLOW: I'll be watching from outside, sir. The door will be open in case either of you need me.
(MARLOW hesitates, then exits, leaving door open, stands outside of door.)

TREVOR: *(Pours self a cup of water, crying and barely able to talk.)* My wife was in that health clinic.

BAILEY: Tracker? I don't know what you are talking about. Swear to God . . . Is Teanna okay?

TREVOR: *(Throws water in BAILEY'S face and grabs BAILEY'S collar.)* Don't speak my wife's name. Never. You got it, fucker?

(MARLOW steps into doorway. TREVOR sees MARLOW and he lets go of BAILEY. Moves to bench.)

BAILEY: *(Nods, pauses.)* Is she okay?

TREVOR: We worded the headlines precisely like you said. Used the exact fonts you dictated. And now three buildings blew up.

BAILEY: What do you mean?

TREVOR: Three fuckin' buildings blew up. You know nothing about that?

BAILEY: Why would I bomb a health clinic? I'm trying to protect health clinics.

TREVOR: I think, Bailey, that your health care legislation was a decoy. Another way to stall and play with us while you and "your people" do more damage.

BAILEY: No, Tracker . . . I swear.
(Stands.)
I swear on Mex.

TREVOR: *(Pause.)* Okay . . . If that's the case . . . You're saying we have a new situation.

BAILEY: *(Nods.)* Swear on Mex.

TREVOR: Fuck!
(Pause.)
Someone's copying the evil sickness you started.
(Stands.)
A new situation.

(TREVOR motions calmly for MARLOW to enter. MARLOW enters and stands silently. TREVOR walks toward Observation Room, but stops with his back to BAILEY.)

TREVOR: Your leukemia is back. You kept that from me.

BAILEY: A few months ago . . . Will I see you again?

TREVOR: *(Pauses, then turns to Bailey.)* When you see Mex? Tell him, "Go Raiders," for me.

BAILEY: Thanks, Tracker. Mex'll like that . . . God will see us through.

(TREVOR nods to MARLOW to escort BAILEY out.)

BAILEY: Goodbye, Tracker.

(TREVOR stares blankly at BAILEY as MARLOW hoods him. BAILEY and MARLOW exit as TREVOR sits in chair with exhaustion.)

FINCH: *(Enters Interrogation Room.)* I told you to wait. Not move out of that chair.

TREVOR: I needed a bit more Intel.

FINCH: "A bit more Intel?" Uh-huh. Using that phrase means you're treading in deep shit.

TREVOR: Bailey's not involved in the new bombings.

FINCH: I know. Here's our latest "intel."
(Hands papers to Trevor.)
You were right. We have a "new situation."

TREVOR: You were watching Bailey and me?

FINCH: A group took responsibility for today's bombings. They call themselves "Down with Big Business." "DBB."

TREVOR: How clever.

FINCH: Some people here insist Bailey masterminded these new bombings.

TREVOR: Martin and Bledsoe?

FINCH: Imagine that.

TREVOR: Do they plan to rough him up again?

FINCH: It'll make those two big, tough men feel better.

TREVOR: I expect so . . . Did you get my maple donut?

FINCH: Krispy Kreme can't make deliveries.

TREVOR: No fuel?

FINCH: *(Disheartened.)* That. And no flour, no sugar.

TREVOR: *(Mumbles.)* It's all unraveling.

FINCH: *(Steps toward exit, stops, turns to TREVOR.)* Teanna called me.

(TREVOR gestures, "Now what else can go wrong?")

FINCH: Listen, Tracker. Go with her to New Zealand. Otherwise, all of this . . . It never ends.
(Lost in thought to herself.)
You find yourself with a home you never see, vacations you never take, kids you wished you knew.
(To Trevor.)
Two choices.

TREVOR: Both wolves are hungry.

FINCH: What's that?

TREVOR: *(Shakes head.)* Nothing.

(FINCH nods, pauses, and then exits.)

(TREVOR walks to switches by door and turns off main lights, leaving only interrogation lamp on. Walks back to bench. Puts on jacket, pulls wedding ring out of pocket, examines it. Sits Native-American style on the floor beneath the lamp. Sets ring on the floor and looks at it. Looks into light directly overhead. Speaks with sign language for, "Grandfather? Wolves many dangerous." He repeats the gesture three times for "dangerous" but the third time he leaves his hand on his chest. Bows head and cries.)

(Lights to black.)

FINALE

About the Authors

Travis Teffner

Travis Teffner is a stage and film actor, from Hendersonville, North Carolina. He has also co-authored alongside DC Fidler on the play, *Santee Delta* and authored the play, *Over Before It Began.*

DC Fidler

A native of the South, DC Fidler has combined a career in academic psychiatry and cultural psychiatry with a lifetime of playwriting, acting, directing, composing music, and teaching creative writing and the dramatic arts.

He studied theatre, writing, chemistry, medicine, and psychiatry at the University of North Carolina at Chapel Hill, where he served on the faculty. He later served on the faculty at West Virginia University, teaching cultural psychiatry, clinical psychiatry, and acting.

A licensed psychiatrist, DC Fidler has lived and worked with the Alutiiq tribe in Akhiok, Alaska, the Al Moqbali Bedouin tribe near Sohar, Oman, the Kalkadoon Aboriginal Tribe in the outback of Queensland, Australia, and the Te Tau Ihu Maori Tribes on the South Island of New Zealand.

He began his acting career in outdoor dramas, summer stock theatre, and local films and television at age ten. He has written scripts and composed music for over fifty medical educational videos at UNC-CH and WVU. He has written seventeen plays that have been produced in various community theatres and universities across North Carolina, Virginia, and West Virginia, as well as St. Louis, Sacramento, San Diego, Los Angeles, Boston, Chicago, and New York City.

He consulted and appeared in educational productions for HBO, ABC, and PBS and performed in numerous stage plays including: *Hope is the Thing with Feathers, Night of January 16th, Thieves' Carnival, Blood Wedding, Our Town, A Life in the Theatre,* and *Fool for Love.*

Presently, he is a scriptwriter, film director, and medical consultant for educational films using professional actors to demonstrate mental health issues. In addition, he is an active member of the Dramatists Guild of America and the Charlotte Writers' Club.

Fidler previously chaired the Video Committee for the American Psychiatric Association and served as President of the Association for Academic Psychiatry. In 2003, he was inducted as a Fellow of the Royal College of Physicians of Ireland. He serves on the Arts and Humanities Committee for the Group for the Advancement of Psychiatry where he is co-producing a video series on the History of Psychiatry, and using the arts to teach people about mental health.

He is author of the textbook, *Psychiatry for Actors: Using Psychiatric Principles to Build Characters,* and author of the novel, *Boogieban.*

Plays by DC Fidler and Travis Teffner
- Elk and Wolf
- Santee Delta
- Moon Bugs

Plays by DC Fidler
- Voices in the Woods
- Guilt by Association (With RJ Casey)
- Three Diaries
- Master William Bowlinggreen and Company
- Shiraz
- The Anniversary of Miss Nanette Pringle
- School Children Hiding Under Desks
- Grams
- Camp Uni
- Boogieban (Two-Actor Version)
- Boogieban (Seven-Actor Version)
- Ahulaqs
- Celtic Crossing
- Stone Touchin'
- Daugherty Park Merry-Go-Round
- La Dynastie
- Gyges Solution
- Persons
- Cruise
- Mobile to Where
- Oman Truce
- Second Amendment
- The Greek God Club
- Four X
- Microscopic Misconceptions
- Drone Guns

Plays by Travis Teffner
- Over Before It Began
- Grilling

Musicals by DC Fidler
- Pied Piper
- Healer Man
- Medicine Show